VIOLET STRANGE IN

The Golden Slipper

ANNA KATHARINE GREEN

PROBLEM 1

first published in 1915

"She's here! I thought she would be. She's one of the three young ladies you see in the right-hand box near the proscenium."

The gentleman thus addressed—a man of middle age and a member of the most exclusive clubs— turned his opera glass toward the spot designated, and in some astonishment retorted:

"She? Why those are the Misses Pratt and—"

"Miss Violet Strange; no other."

"And do you mean to say—"

"I do—"

"That yon silly little chit, whose father I know, whose fortune

I know, who is seen everywhere, and who is called one of the season's belles is an agent of yours; a—a—"

"No names here, please. You want a mystery solved. It is not a matter for the police—that is, as yet,—and so you come to me, and when I ask for the facts, I find that women and only women are involved, and that these women are not only young but one and all of the highest society. Is it a man's work to go to the bottom of a combination like this? No. Sex against sex, and, if possible, youth against youth. Happily, I know such a person—a girl of gifts and extraordinarily well placed for the purpose. Why she uses her talents in this direction—why, with means enough to play the part natural to her as a successful debutante, she consents to occupy herself with social and other mysteries, you must ask her, not me. Enough that I promise you her aid if you want it. That is, if you can interest her. She will not work otherwise."

Mr. Driscoll again raised his opera glass.

"But it's a comedy face," he commented. "It's hard to associate intellectuality with such quaintness of expression. Are you sure of her discretion?"

"Whom is she with?"

"Abner Pratt, his wife, and daughters."

"Is he a man to entrust his affairs unadvisedly?"

"Abner Pratt! Do you mean to say that she is anything more to him than his daughters' guest?"

"Judge. You see how merry they are. They were in deep

trouble yesterday. You are witness to a celebration."

"And she?"

"Don't you observe how they are loading her with attentions? She's too young to rouse such interest in a family of notably unsympathetic temperament for any other reason than that of gratitude."

"It's hard to believe. But if what you hint is true, secure me an opportunity at once of talking to this youthful marvel. My affair is serious. The dinner I have mentioned comes off in three days and—"

"I know. I recognize your need; but I think you had better enter Mr. Pratt's box without my intervention. Miss Strange's value to us will be impaired the moment her connection with us is discovered."

"Ah, there's Ruthven! He will take me to Mr. Pratt's box," remarked Driscoll as the curtain fell on the second act. "Any suggestions before I go?"

"Yes, and an important one. When you make your bow, touch your left shoulder with your right hand. It is a signal. She may respond to it; but if she does not, do not be discouraged. One of her idiosyncrasies is a theoretical dislike of her work. But once she gets interested, nothing will hold her back. That's all, except this. In no event give away her secret. That's part of the compact, you remember."

Driscoll nodded and left his seat for Ruthven's box. When the curtain rose for the third time he could be seen sitting with the Misses Pratt and their vivacious young friend. A widower and still on the right side of fifty, his presence there did not pass unnoted, and curiosity was rife among certain onlookers as to which of the twin belles was responsible for this change in his well-known habits. Unfortunately, no opportunity was given him for showing. Other and younger men had followed his lead into the box, and they saw him forced upon the good graces of the fascinating but inconsequent Miss Strange whose rapid fire of talk he was hardly of a temperament to appreciate.

Did he appear dissatisfied? Yes; but only one person in the opera house knew why. Miss

Strange had shown no comprehension of or sympathy with his errand. Though she chatted amiably enough between duets and trios, she gave him no opportunity to express his wishes though she knew them well enough, owing to the signal he had given her.

This might be in character but it hardly suited his views; and, being a man of resolution, he took advantage of an absorbing minute on the stage to lean forward and whisper in her ear:

"It's my daughter for whom I request your services; as fine a girl as any in this house. Give me a hearing. You certainly can manage it."

She was a small, slight woman whose naturally quaint appearance was accentuated by the extreme simplicity of her attire. In the tier upon tier of boxes rising before his eyes, no other personality could vie with hers in strangeness, or in the illusive quality of her ever-changing expression. She was vivacity incarnate and, to the ordinary observer, light as thistledown in fibre and in feeling. But not to all. To those who watched her long, there came moments—say when the music rose to heights of greatness—when the mouth so given over to laughter took on curves of the rarest sensibility, and a woman's lofty soul shone through her odd, bewildering features.

Driscoll had noted this, and consequently awaited her reply in secret hope.

It came in the form of a question and only after an instant's display of displeasure or possibly of pure nervous irritability.

"What has she done?"

"Nothing. But slander is in the air, and any day it may ripen into public accusation."

"Accusation of what?" Her tone was almost pettish.

"Of—of theft," he murmured. "On a great scale," he

emphasized, as the music rose to a crash.

"Jewels?"

"Inestimable ones. They are always returned by somebody. People say, by me."

"Ah!" The little lady's hands grew steady,— they had been fluttering all over her lap. "I will see you to-morrow morning at my father's house," she presently observed; and turned her full attention to the stage.

Some three days after this Mr. Driscoll opened his house on the Hudson to notable guests. He had not desired the publicity of such an event, nor the opportunity it gave for an increase of

the scandal secretly
in circulation against
his daughter. But the
Ambassador and his
wife were foreign and
any evasion of the
promised hospitality
would be sure to
be misunderstood;
so the scheme was
carried forward
though with less
eclat than possibly
was expected.

Among the lesser guests, who were mostly young and well acquainted with the house and its hospitality, there was one unique figure,— that of the lively Miss Strange, who, if personally unknown to Miss Driscoll, was so gifted with the qualities which tell on an occasion of this kind, that the stately young hostess hailed her presence with very obvious gratitude.

The manner of their first meeting was singular, and of great interest to one of them at least. Miss Strange had come in an automobile and had been shown her room; but there was nobody to accompany her down-stairs afterward, and, finding herself alone in the great hall, she naturally moved toward the library, the door of which stood ajar. She had pushed this door half open before she noticed that the room was already occupied. As a consequence, she was made the unexpected observer of a beautiful picture of youth and love.

A young man and a young woman were standing together in the glow of a blazing wood-fire. No word was to be heard, but in their faces, eloquent with passion, there shone something so deep and true that the chance intruder hesitated on the threshold, eager to lay this picture away in her

mind with the other
lovely and tragic
memories now fast
accumulating there.
Then she drew back,
and readvancing
with a less noiseless
foot, came into
the full presence
of Captain Holliday
drawn up in all the
pride of his military
rank beside Alicia,
the accomplished
daughter of the
house, who, if under

a shadow as many whispered, wore that shadow as some women wear a crown.

Miss Strange was struck with admiration, and turned upon them the brightest facet of her vivacious nature all the time she was saying to herself: "Does she know why I am here? Or does she look upon me only as an additional guest foisted upon her by a thoughtless parent?"

There was nothing in the manner of her cordial but composed young hostess to show, and Miss Strange, with but one thought in mind since she had caught the light of feeling on the two faces confronting her, took the first opportunity that offered of running over the facts given her by Mr. Driscoll, to see if any reconcilement were possible between them and an innocence in which she must henceforth believe.

They were certainly of a most damaging nature.

Miss Driscoll and four other young ladies of her own station in life had formed themselves, some two years before, into a coterie of five, called The Inseparables. They lunched together, rode together, visited together. So close was the bond and their mutual dependence so evident, that it came to be the custom to invite the whole five whenever the size of the function warranted it. In fact, it was far from an uncommon occurrence to see them grouped at receptions or following one another down the aisles of churches or through the mazes of the dance at balls or assemblies. And no

one demurred at
this, for they were
all handsome and
attractive girls, till it
began to be noticed
that, coincident with
their presence, some
article of value was
found missing from
the dressing-room
or from the tables
where wedding gifts
were displayed.
Nothing was safe
where they went, and
though, in the course

of time, each article found its way back to its owner in a manner as mysterious as its previous abstraction, the scandal grew and, whether with good reason or bad, finally settled about the person of Miss Driscoll, who was the showiest, least pecuniarily tempted, and most dignified in manner and speech of them all.

Some instances had been given by way of further enlightenment. This is one: A theatre party was in progress. There were twelve in the party, five of whom were the Inseparables. In the course of the last act, another lady—in fact, their chaperon—missed her handkerchief, an almost priceless bit of lace. Positive that she had brought it with her into the box, she caused a careful search, but without the least success. Recalling certain whispers she had heard, she noted which of the five girls were with her in the box. They were Miss Driscoll, Miss Hughson, Miss Yates, and Miss Benedict.

Miss West sat in the box adjoining.

A fortnight later this handkerchief reappeared—and where? Among the cushions of a yellow satin couch in her own drawing-room. The Inseparables had just made their call and the three who had sat on the couch were Miss Driscoll,

Miss Hughson, and Miss Benedict.

The next instance seemed to point still more insistently toward the lady already named. Miss Yates had an expensive present to buy, and the whole five Inseparables went in an imposing group to Tiffany's. A tray of rings was set before them.

All examined and eagerly fingered the stock out of which Miss Yates presently chose a finely set emerald. She was leading her friends away when the clerk suddenly whispered in her ear, "I miss one of the rings." Dismayed beyond speech, she turned and consulted the faces of her four companions who stared back at her with immovable serenity. But one of them was paler than usual, and this lady (it was Miss Driscoll) held her hands in her muff and did not offer to take them out. Miss Yates, whose father had completed a big "deal" the week before, wheeled round upon the clerk. "Charge it! charge it at its full value," said she. "I buy both the rings."

And in three weeks the purloined ring came back to her, in a box of violets with no name attached.

The third instance was a recent one, and had come to Mr. Driscoll's ears directly from the lady suffering the loss. She was a woman of uncompromising integrity, who felt it her duty to make known to this gentleman the following facts: She had just left a studio reception, and was standing at the curb waiting for a taxicab to draw up, when a small boy—a street arab—darted toward her from the other side of the street,

and thrusting into
her hand something
small and hard,
cried breathlessly
as he slipped away,
"It's yours, ma'am;
you dropped it."
Astonished, for
she had not been
conscious of any
loss, she looked
down at her treasure
trove and found
it to be a small
medallion which she
sometimes wore on

a chain at her belt. But she had not worn it that day, nor any day for weeks. Then she remembered. She had worn it a month before to a similar reception at this same studio. A number of young girls had stood about her admiring it—she remembered well who they were; the Inseparables, of course, and to please

them she had slipped
it from its chain.
Then something
had happened,—
something which
diverted her
attention entirely,—
and she had gone
home without the
medallion; had, in
fact, forgotten it,
only to recall its
loss now. Placing
it in her bag, she
looked hastily about
her. A crowd was

at her back; nothing to be distinguished there. But in front, on the opposite side of the street, stood a club-house, and in one of its windows she perceived a solitary figure looking out. It was that of Miss Driscoll's father. He could imagine her conclusion.

In vain he denied all knowledge of the

matter. She told him other stories which had come to her ears of thefts as mysterious, followed by restorations as peculiar as this one, finishing with, "It is your daughter, and people are beginning to say so."

And Miss Strange, brooding over these instances, would have said the same, but for Miss Driscoll's absolute serenity of demeanour and complete abandonment to love. These seemed incompatible with guilt; these, whatever the appearances, proclaimed innocence—an innocence she was here to prove if fortune favoured and the really guilty person's madness should again break forth.

For madness it would be and nothing less, for any hand, even the most experienced, to draw attention to itself by a repetition of old tricks on an occasion so marked. Yet because it would take madness, and madness knows no law, she prepared herself for the contingency under a mask of girlish smiles which made her at once the delight and astonishment of her watchful and uneasy host.

With the exception of the diamonds worn by the Ambassadress, there was but one jewel of consequence to be seen at the dinner that night; but how great was that consequence and with what splendour it invested the snowy neck it adorned!

Miss Strange, in compliment to the noble foreigners, had put on one of her family heirlooms—a filigree pendant of extraordinary sapphires which had once belonged to Marie Antoinette. As its beauty flashed upon the women, and its value struck the host, the latter could not restrain himself from casting an anxious eye about the board in search of some token of the cupidity with which one person there must welcome this unexpected sight.

Naturally his first glance fell upon

Alicia, seated opposite to him at the other end of the table. But her eyes were elsewhere, and her smile for Captain Holliday, and the father's gaze travelled on, taking up each young girl's face in turn. All were contemplating Miss Strange and her jewels, and the cheeks of one were flushed and those of the others pale, but whether with dread or longing who could tell. Struck with foreboding, but alive to his duty as host, he forced his glances away, and did not even allow himself to question the motive or the wisdom of the temptation thus offered.

Two hours later and the girls were

all in one room. It was a custom of the Inseparables to meet for a chat before retiring, but always alone and in the room of one of their number. But this was a night of innovations; Violet was not only included, but the meeting was held in her room. Her way with girls was even more fruitful of result than her way with men. They might laugh at her, criticize her or even call her names significant of disdain, but they never left her long to herself or missed an opportunity to make the most of her irrepressible chatter.

Her satisfaction at entering this charmed circle did not take from her piquancy, and story after story fell from her lips, as she fluttered about, now here now there, in her endless preparations for retirement. She had taken off her historic pendant after it had been duly admired and handled by all present, and, with the careless confidence of an assured ownership, thrown it down upon the end of her dresser, which, by the way, projected very close to the open window.

"Are you going to leave your jewel there?" whispered a voice in her ear as a burst of laughter rang out in response to one of her sallies.

Turning, with a simulation of round-eyed wonder,

she met Miss Hughson's earnest gaze with the careless rejoinder, "What's the harm?" and went on with her story with all the reckless ease of a perfectly thoughtless nature.

Miss Hughson abandoned her protest. How could she explain her reasons for it to one apparently uninitiated in the scandal associated with their especial clique.

Yes, she left the jewel there; but she locked her door and quickly, so that they must all have heard her before reaching their rooms. Then she crossed to the window, which, like all on this side, opened on a balcony running the length of the house. She was aware of this balcony, also of the fact that only young ladies slept in the corridor communicating with it. But she was not quite sure that this one corridor accommodated them all. If one of them should room elsewhere! (Miss Driscoll, for instance). But no! the anxiety displayed for the safety of her jewel precluded that supposition. Their hostess, if none of the others, was within access of this room and its open window. But how about the rest? Perhaps the lights would tell. Eagerly the little schemer looked forth, and let her glances travel down the full length of the balcony. Two separate beams of light shot across it as she looked, and presently another, and, after some waiting, a fourth. But the fifth failed to appear. This troubled her, but not seriously. Two of the girls might be sleeping in one bed.

Drawing her shade, she finished her preparations for the night; then with her kimono on, lifted the pendant and thrust it into a small box she had taken from her trunk. A curious smile, very unlike any she had shown to man or woman that day, gave a sarcastic lift to her lips, as with a slow and thoughtful manipulation of her dainty fingers she moved the jewel about in this small receptacle and then returned it, after one quick examining glance, to the very spot on the dresser from which she had taken it. "If only the madness is great enough!" that smile seemed to say. Truly, it was much to hope for, but a chance is a chance; and comforting herself with the thought, Miss Strange put out her light, and, with a hasty raising of the shade she had previously pulled down, took a final look at the prospect.

Its aspect made her shudder. A low fog was rising from the meadows in the far distance, and its ghostliness under the moon woke all sorts of uncanny images in her excited mind. To escape them she crept into bed where she lay with her eyes on the end of her dresser. She had closed that half of the French window over which she had drawn the shade; but she had left ajar the one giving free access to the jewels; and when she was not watching the scintillation of her sapphires in the moonlight, she was dwelling in fixed attention on this narrow opening.

But nothing happened, and two o'clock, then three o'clock struck, without a dimming of the blue scintillations on the end of her dresser. Then she suddenly sat up. Not that she heard anything new, but that a thought had come to her. "If an attempt is made," so she murmured softly to herself, "it will be by—" She did not finish. Something— she could not call it sound—set her heart beating tumultuously, and listening—listening—

watching—watching—
she followed in her
imagination the
approach down the
balcony of an almost
inaudible step, not
daring to move
herself, it seemed
so near, but waiting
with eyes fixed, for
the shadow which
must fall across the
shade she had failed
to raise over that
half of the swinging

window she had so carefully left shut.

At length she saw it projecting slowly across the slightly illuminated surface. Formless, save for the outreaching hand, it passed the casement's edge, nearing with pauses and hesitations the open gap beyond through which the neglected sapphires beamed with steady lustre. Would she ever see the hand itself appear between the dresser and the window frame? Yes, there it comes,— small, delicate, and startlingly white, threading that gap—darting with the suddenness of a serpent's tongue toward the dresser and disappearing again with the pendant in its clutch.

As she realizes this,—she is but young, you know,—as she sees her bait taken and the hardly expected event fulfilled, her pent-up breath sped forth in a sigh which sent the intruder flying, and so startled herself that she sank back in terror on her pillow.

The breakfast-call had sounded its musical chimes through the halls. The Ambassador and his wife had responded, so had most of the young gentlemen and ladies, but the daughter of the house was not amongst them, nor Miss Strange, whom one would naturally expect to see down first of all.

These two absences puzzled Mr. Driscoll. What might they not portend? But his suspense, at least in one regard, was short. Before his guests were well seated, Miss Driscoll entered from the terrace in company with Captain Holliday. In her arms she carried a huge bunch of roses and was looking very beautiful. Her father's heart warmed at the sight. No shadow from the night rested upon her.

But Miss Strange!— where was she? He could not feel quite easy till he knew.

"Have any of you seen Miss Strange?" he asked, as they sat down at table. And his eyes sought the Inseparables.

Five lovely heads were shaken, some carelessly, some wonderingly, and one, with a quick, forced smile. But he was in no mood to discriminate, and he had beckoned one of the servants to him, when a step was heard at the door and the delinquent slid in and took her place, in a shamefaced manner suggestive of a cause deeper than mere tardiness. In fact, she had what might be called a frightened air, and stared into her plate, avoiding every eye, which was certainly not natural to her. What did it mean? and why, as she made a poor attempt at eating, did four of the Inseparables exchange glances of doubt and dismay and then concentrate their looks upon his daughter? That Alicia failed to notice this, but sat abloom above her roses now fastened in a great bunch upon her breast, offered him some comfort, yet, for all the volubility of his chief guests, the meal was a great trial to his patience, as well as a poor preparation for the hour when, the noble pair gone, he stepped into the library to find Miss Strange awaiting him with one hand behind her back and a piteous look on her infantile features.

"O, Mr. Driscoll," she began,—and then he saw that a group of anxious girls hovered in her rear—"my pendant! my beautiful pendant! It is gone!

Somebody reached in from the balcony and took it from my dresser in the night. Of course, it was to frighten me; all of the girls told me not to leave it there. But I—I cannot make them give it back, and papa is so particular about this jewel that I'm afraid to go home. Won't you tell them it's no joke, and see that I get it again. I won't be so careless another time."

Hardly believing his eyes, hardly believing his ears,—she was so perfectly the spoiled child detected in a fault—he looked sternly about upon the girls and bade them end the jest and produce the gems at once.

But not one of them spoke, and not one of them moved; only his daughter grew pale until the roses seemed a mockery, and the steady stare of her large eyes was almost too much for him to bear.

The anguish of this gave asperity to his manner, and in a strange, hoarse tone he loudly cried:

"One of you did this. Which? If it was you, Alicia, speak. I am in no mood for nonsense. I want to know whose foot traversed the balcony and whose hand abstracted these jewels."

A continued silence, deepening into painful embarrassment for all. Mr. Driscoll eyed them in ill-concealed anguish, then turning to Miss Strange was still further thrown off his balance by seeing her pretty head droop and her gaze fall in confusion.

"Oh! it's easy enough to tell whose foot traversed the balcony," she murmured. "It left this behind." And drawing forward her hand, she held out to view a small gold-coloured slipper. "I found it outside my window," she explained. "I hoped I should not have to show it."

A gasp of uncontrollable feeling from the surrounding group of girls, then absolute stillness.

"I fail to recognize it," observed Mr. Driscoll, taking it in his hand. "Whose slipper is this?" he asked in a manner not to be gainsaid.

Still no reply, then as he continued to eye the girls one after another a voice—the last he expected to hear—spoke and his daughter cried:

"It is mine. But it was not I who walked in it down the balcony."

"Alicia!"

A month's apprehension was in that cry. The silence, the pent-up emotion brooding in the air was intolerable. A fresh young laugh broke it.

"Oh," exclaimed a roguish voice, "I knew that you were all in it! But the especial one who wore the slipper and grabbed the pendant cannot hope to hide herself. Her finger-tips will give her away."

Amazement on every face and a convulsive movement in one half-hidden hand.

"You see," the airy little being went on, in her light way, "I have some awfully funny tricks. I am always being scolded for them, but somehow I don't improve. One is to keep my jewelry bright with a strange foreign paste an old Frenchwoman once gave me in Paris. It's of a vivid red, and stains the fingers dreadfully if you don't take care. Not even water will take it off, see mine. I used that paste on my pendant last night just after you left me, and being awfully sleepy I didn't stop to rub it off. If your finger-tips are not red, you never touched the pendant, Miss Driscoll. Oh, see! They are as white as milk.

"But some one took the sapphires, and I owe that person a scolding, as well as myself. Was it you, Miss Hughson?

You, Miss Yates? or—" and here she paused before Miss West, "Oh, you have your gloves on! You are the guilty one!" and her laugh rang out like a peal of bells, robbing her next sentence of even a suggestion of sarcasm. "Oh, what a sly-boots!" she cried. "How you have deceived me! Whoever would have thought you to be the one to play the mischief!"

Who indeed! Of all the five, she was the one who was considered absolutely immune from suspicion ever since the night Mrs. Barnum's handkerchief had been taken, and she not in the box. Eyes which had surveyed

Miss Driscoll askance now rose in wonder toward hers, and failed to fall again because of the stoniness into which her delicately-carved features had settled.

"Miss West, I know you will be glad to remove your gloves; Miss Strange certainly has a right to know her special tormentor," spoke up her host in as natural a voice as his great relief would allow.

But the cold, half-frozen woman remained without a movement. She was not deceived by the banter of the moment. She knew that to all of the others, if not to Peter Strange's odd little daughter, it was the thief who was being spotted and brought thus hilariously to light. And her eyes grew hard, and her lips grey, and she failed to unglove the hands upon which all glances were concentrated.

"You do not need to see my hands; I confess to taking the pendant."

"Caroline!"

A heart overcome by shock had thrown up this cry. Miss West eyed her bosom-friend disdainfully.

"Miss Strange has called it a jest," she coldly commented. "Why should you suggest anything of a graver character?"

Alicia brought thus to bay, and by one she had trusted most, stepped

quickly forward,
and quivering with
vague doubts, aghast
before unheard-of
possibilities,
she tremulously
remarked:

"We did not sleep
together last night.
You had to come into
my room to get my
slippers. Why did you
do this? What was in
your mind, Caroline?"

A steady look, a low laugh choked with many emotions answered her.

"Do you want me to reply, Alicia? Or shall we let it pass?"

"Answer!"

It was Mr. Driscoll who spoke. Alicia had shrunk back, almost to where a little figure was cowering with wide eyes fixed in something like terror on the aroused father's face.

"Then hear me," murmured the girl, entrapped and suddenly desperate. "I wore Alicia's slippers and I took the jewels, because it was time that an end should come to your mutual dissimulation. The love I once felt for

her she has herself
deliberately killed.
I had a lover—she
took him. I had faith
in life, in honour,
and in friendship.
She destroyed all. A
thief—she has dared
to aspire to him! And
you condoned her
fault. You, with your
craven restoration of
her booty, thought
the matter cleared
and her a fit mate

for a man of highest honour."

"Miss West,"—no one had ever heard that tone in Mr. Driscoll's voice before, "before you say another word calculated to mislead these ladies, let me say that this hand never returned any one's booty or had anything to do with the restoration of any abstracted article.

You have been caught in a net, Miss West, from which you cannot escape by slandering my innocent daughter."

"Innocent!" All the tragedy latent in this peculiar girl's nature blazed forth in the word. "Alicia, face me. Are you innocent? Who took the Dempsey corals, and that diamond from the Tiffany tray?"

"It is not necessary for Alicia to answer," the father interposed with not unnatural heat. "Miss West stands self-convicted."

"How about Lady Paget's scarf? I was not there that night."

"You are a woman of wiles. That could

be managed by one bent on an elaborate scheme of revenge."

"And so could the abstraction of Mrs. Barnum's five-hundred-dollar handkerchief by one who sat in the next box," chimed in Miss Hughson, edging away from the friend to whose honour she would have pinned her faith an hour before. "I remember now seeing her lean over the railing to adjust the old lady's shawl."

With a start, Caroline West turned a tragic gaze upon the speaker.

"You think me guilty of all because of what I did last night?"

"Why shouldn't I?"

"And you, Anna?"

"Alicia has my sympathy," murmured Miss Benedict.

Yet the wild girl persisted.

"But I have told you my provocation. You cannot believe that I am guilty of her sin; not if you look at her as I am looking now."

But their glances hardly followed her pointing finger.

Her friends—
the comrades of
her youth, the
Inseparables with
their secret oath—
one and all held
themselves aloof,
struck by the perfidy
they were only just
beginning to take in.
Smitten with despair,
for these girls were
her life, she gave one
wild leap and sank
on her knees before
Alicia.

"O speak!" she began. "Forgive me, and—"

A tremble seized her throat; she ceased to speak and let fall her partially uplifted hands. The cheery sound of men's voices had drifted in from the terrace, and the figure of Captain Holliday could be seen passing by. The shudder which shook Caroline West communicated itself to Alicia Driscoll, and the former rising quickly, the two women surveyed each other, possibly for the first time, with open soul and a complete understanding.

"Caroline!" murmured the one.

"Alicia!" pleaded the other.

"Caroline, trust me," said Alicia Driscoll in that moving voice of hers, which more than her beauty caught and retained all hearts. "You have served me ill, but it was not all undeserved. Girls," she went on, eyeing both them and her father with the wistfulness of a breaking heart, "neither Caroline nor myself are worthy of Captain Holliday's love. Caroline has told you her fault, but mine is perhaps a worse one. The ring—the scarf—the diamond pins—I took them all—took them if I did not retain them. A curse has been over my life— the curse of a longing I could not combat. But love was working a change in me. Since

I have known Captain Holliday—but that's all over. I was mad to think I could be happy with such memories in my life. I shall never marry now—or touch jewels again—my own or another's. Father, father, you won't go back on your girl! I couldn't see Caroline suffer for what I have done. You will pardon me and help—help—"

Her voice choked. She flung herself into her father's arms; his head bent over hers, and for an instant not a soul in the room moved. Then Miss Hughson gave a spring and caught her by the hand. "We are inseparable," said she, and kissed the hand, murmuring,

"Now is our time to show it."

Then other lips fell upon those cold and trembling fingers, which seemed to warm under these embraces. And then a tear. It came from the hard eye of Caroline, and remained a sacred secret between the two.

"You have your pendant?"

Mr. Driscoll's suffering eye shone down on Violet Strange's uplifted face as she advanced to say good-bye preparatory to departure.

"Yes," she acknowledged, "but hardly, I fear, your gratitude."

And the answer astonished her.

"I am not sure that the real Alicia will not make her father happier than the unreal one has ever done."

"And Captain Holliday?"

"He may come to feel the same."

"Then I do not quit in disgrace?"

"You depart with my thanks."

When a certain personage was told of the success of Miss Strange's latest manoeuvre, he remarked: "The little one progresses. We shall have to give her a case of prime importance next."

ABOUT THE AUTHOR

In 1887, a decade before Sherlock Holmes, Anna Katharine Green wrote her first detective story and began her genre defining career. Born in Brooklyn in 1846, she defied a male dominated field and pioneered many conventions of mysteries that remain today.

ABOUT THE COVER

The image on the cover is adapted from a lithograph by the Austrian-Czech artist Alphonse Mucha entitled, "Flirt". It was made sometime between 1895-1900.

VIOLET STRANGE RETURNS IN THE SECOND BULLET

WHAT WE'RE ABOUT

I made the first Super Large Print books for my grandma. She needed books she could keep reading as her glaucoma and macular degeneration advanced. I used a font originally made for people with dyslexia, because the letters are bold and easy to distinguish. The books are set

at 30 pt font, twice
the size of traditional
Large Print. Being
able to read again
was life changing.

Digital reading was
too frustrating for
my grandma. And it
could never offer the
pleasures she had
always associated
with reading. The
peaceful rhythm
of turning a page.
The satisfaction in

knowing a story has "this much left". And the comforting memories of adventure, companionship, and revelation she felt when seeing the cover of her favorite book. Part of what makes reading so relaxing and grounding is the tactile experience. I hope these books can bring joy to those who want to keep reading and to those who've never had the pleasure of curling up with a page turner.

Please let me know if you have any requests for new titles. To leave feedback and to see the complete and constantly updating catalog, please visit:

superlargeprint.com

MORE BOOKS AT:

superlargeprint.com

KEEP ON READING!

ISBN 9781087268194

Made in the USA
Middletown, DE
28 March 2021

36361573R00076